Short Sweetz 1

High Stakes

Robin Martin

Published by Bennett Lane Press 2020

www.robinmartinthomas.com

Disclaimer
Every effort has been made to ensure that this book is free from error or omissions. Information provided is of general nature only and should not be considered legal or financial advice. The intent is to offer a variety of information to the reader. However, the author, publisher, editor or their agents or representatives shall not accept responsibility for any loss or inconvenience caused to a person or organisation relying on this information.

Book cover design and formatting services by Self-PublishingLab.com

ISBN:
978-0-9946465-8-3 (pbk)
978-0-9946465-9-0 (e-bk)

I

Friday

6:30am

The glass doors slid open. As I scurried into the silent lobby, I glanced at my watch. An hour before most people trickled in and two hours before official starting time. Good. I would have cleared my desk, made the first few calls and have a coffee on Shelley's desk, waiting for her when she arrived at 8:15. Points to me. I needed them. Pete had stayed late every night this week and was already looking like the blue-eyed boy. But he wasn't an early riser. I smiled as I stepped in the lift.

6:40am

The office was quiet with only the distant hum of a vacuum cleaner. The file I'd nearly finished last night, before exhaustion had numbed my brain, was still waiting for me. She'd wanted it like, yesterday. As if. Shelley never tired asking for the impossible. But she'd get it this morning on her desk, with the coffee. I'd even tie it in red ribbon if it would make her happy.

6:53am

Was it too early to call the last supplier? It was nearly 8:00 in Sydney.

6:55am

I slammed the receiver down. Who the hell isn't at work by nearly 8:00? I'd try again in five minutes. That's all I needed, one price, and then it was done. Time to grab a coffee. My third since 5:30, but I needed the caffeine jolt.

7:30am

At last, success. Wonder he keeps his job with the hours he keeps. Ze file iz done! Decided against the red ribbon. Shel has no sense of humour. God, here comes Pete. Never mind. Paste smile on face.

'Morning, Pete.'

'You're in early.'

'Nah, not really. Only just got in.' Tell the enemy nothing. I slid from my desk with the file.

'Finished that one at last, eh?'

He is one smartass. He knew it was due in yesterday.

'No probs. Did it yesterday. Just checking it. You know what she's like.' He was standing uncomfortably close. I hated that he was taller than me, even when I was wearing heels.

'Actually, I have always found Shelley quite reasonable. As long as you do the work, keep to schedule, she's happy.'

'Oh yeah, I know what you mean. She can be understanding; even when you make mistakes, like that estimate you did last week. Even though it was a few ks out, she really stood by you.' I had the satisfaction of seeing his face deepen two shades. Smug Pommie B.

'Well, I guess you would know. If you hurry, you can just pop that file on her desk and she'll think you finished it yesterday.' He winked at me and sauntered off to his cubicle. My fingers tightened around the paperweight on my desk.

7:40am

The swing doors to the office burst open and Shelley made her entrance, three inch heels clacking, Dior silk scarf flowing behind and manicured red nails digging into the takeaway coffee. Double shot black. No sugar.

Damn, I still didn't have the file on her desk and she already had her coffee. Why did she have to pick this morning to come in earlier than usual? That little squabble with smartass had taken up valuable time.

'Good, you're both here. Pete, Kate, my office – now.'

Clutching my file, I took a deep breath and followed in the wake of her Chanel perfume. Naturally, Pete was at the door of her office before both of us, grinning and opening the door.

With a flick of her hand, she motioned for us to sit. She walked to her desk and stood for a moment, looking out the window and sipping her coffee. No indication yet whether her mood was up or down. That was Shelley all over — cool, analytical, deadly.

I quickly placed the file on her desk, and then settled back in my chair, ignoring Pete on the other side of me.

She turned and scanned us with her slate grey eyes; then, with a half-smile, sat down. 'I won't beat about the bush. There's a promotion going and you two are being considered.' Pete started gushing gratitude, but she held up a hand to silence him. 'The board meets at the beginning of the month and will make its decision then, based on my recommendation, of course. I'll be looking at all the usual things; top performance, time management, and willingness to go that extra mile. But there's something else too. This new position involves leadership skills, because whoever gets it will be managing a small team of about four to six people. People skills are probably the most important criteria of the lot.'

Says the person who has none, I thought.

'Both of you have what it takes if you put your minds to it. However, you're loners. In early, out late. That's good, folks — but you've got to mix, get to know others, understand what makes them tick. Most importantly you have to get on with each other. Whoever doesn't get the promotion will be on the team of the one who does. So,' she paused and smiled. It sent a chill down my spine. 'I have decided that you'll both work on one project.It'll mean cooperating, understanding each other and watching each other's back.'

So we can stab it. Shush, I told my brain.

'The question now is,' she continued, 'can you do it? I know there's a bit of rivalry between you two. That's fine, that's healthy. But can you put it aside for the greater good of the company? This isn't just about a promotion, this is about an attitude. To get to the top you need to put the business first and yourself last. I don't need to tell you it's a tough world out there. There are opportunities, but only for those who have the guts to take them. Well? Feedback?'

'Brill idea, Shelley. I'd love the opportunity of working with Kate. She's such a little go-getter! I'm sure we'll get on fine.' He flashed me a toothy grin and I forced a grimace in response.

I didn't want to but I had to ask. 'Since we'll be working together, helping each other, how will you be able to decide who is the best?'

'Leave that to me, Kate. By the end of this I'll know who the leader in this relationship is.'

Relationship? Jeez, the only relationship I wanted with that creep was long distance, preferably with several continents between us because I'd kicked his butt that far.

'What's the problem, Kate? You want out of this?'

'No, not at all. I welcome the challenge of working with someone of Pete's calibre. I'm sure we'll both learn a lot.'

'Good. Here's what you're working on.' She tossed a folder over her desk. 'This is the PD policy for the staff. It needs updating. In the current environment, professional development is taking on increasing importance. It's no longer a case of attending a few workshops or seminars that the company puts on. People have to be more proactive. They have to invest some of their own time and resources into furthering their careers — that is if they are interested in becoming valuable employees. I want a total rewrite of the policy and an updated pro forma for every employee to fill in outlining their own plans for PD, along with identification of their strengths, weaknesses, reflections on what they have done well, what they can improve on — that sort of thing. When you've done that, I want you to fill one in for each other. By the end of this you should know each other pretty well. I'll be interested to see the results.'

I tried to keep my jaw from falling open. She was a devious, conniving, sadistic bitch. I reached over to take

the folder before Pete did. 'When do you want it, Shelley?'
I asked.

'Monday.'

Shit, I thought. Today was Friday.

'No problems,' Pete said. 'I've read the policy already
and I have a few ideas. But Kate, you might like to
familiarise yourself with it before we get together.'

I opened my mouth to say something, but Shel gave me
no chance. 'Fine, the sooner you get started the better.' She
waved a dismissive hand at us and picked up the phone.

As I headed out the door, she said, 'And Kate, make
sure this one's on time.' She glanced at the file I had placed
on her desk and then back at me.

I gave her a sickly smile and nodded.

7:55am

I glanced around the nearly full office. Even though
official starting time was 8:30, hardly anyone arrived that
late, except losers. Pete followed me to my desk.

'When do you want to get started?' He was grinning
at me. He thinks he's got it aced, I thought.

'Never,' I said.

'Oh well, saves time. I'll just let Shel know the
decision's been made for her.'

'Shut up, Smartass.'

'Looks like we're off to a good start. Come on, chill. We've got to work together so let's make the best of it. Why don't we read over the policy and bounce a few ideas over lunch.'

'Thought you'd already done that?'

He shrugged his shoulders. 'Yeah, when I first joined Calco. As for ideas, I've always got them in spades.'

'As in shovelling it?' I raised my eyebrows.

'Oh, you are one clever cookie. You can either work with me or not, Kate. I don't give a damn. Just make your mind up. The outcome is going to be the same anyway.'

I took a deep breath, ignoring the last provocative remark. 'Right, let's make one thing clear first, though. No bullshit. We don't like each other, never have. That's a given. But we'll call a truce for now. Let's play it straight up and honest. No games.'

'Agreed.' He held out a hand and I shook it. His hand was firm, warm and his smile looked genuine. I didn't trust him a millimetre.

'OMG, the world's coming to an end. Did I actually see Pete and Kate shake hands?' Mike Carmichael's voice boomed through the office and several curious glances shot our way.

'Shove it, Carmichael. Business only — not that it's any of yours!' I gave him a death stare and he chuckled, and then turned back to his computer.

'Lunch at noon?' Pete asked.

'Yeah, somewhere quiet away from this lot.'

'Meet you at Shannon's then.'

I nodded and he went back to his desk.

I glanced at my watch. 7:59. It wasn't even eight o'clock yet and already it was a lousy day.

9:35am

Nearly through the PD document. Time for coffee number four, which wasn't bad, considering my last one was 6:55. Still couldn't believe what Shel was making me do. I'd rather climb Mt Kosciusko starkers in July. I'd rather swim in shark-infested waters clutching a leaky meat tray. I'd even rather be a contestant on Master Chef and I hate cooking. I walked past Pete's cubicle. His feet were on the desk and he was talking on the phone. He gave me a casual wave as if we were best buddies. What was he up to? Thoughts ricocheted in my head as I got a coffee from the canteen.

'Hey, Kate,' Carmichael's head popped around the corner, 'you got a thing going with Pete?'

I glared at him.

'Just asking.' His pale, freckled face broke into a grin and he ran a hand through his untidy red hair.

'Shelley gave us a project to work on together, is all.' I shrugged.

'Wow, when is World War Three?'

'We're adults. We can be civil.'

He looked at me.

'Well, we can.'

'Sure.' He twisted his cup in his hands.

I turned to head back to my desk.

'Kate?'

'Yeah?'

'I was wondering, you free tonight? You want to have a drink after work? A few of us are going to a new wine bar open on George Street. They've got a guitarist there.'

'Thanks, but I can't make it. I'll probably be working late. Shel wants this thing finished by Monday.'

'Yeah, sure. But it is Friday, you know.'

'As if that matters around here.' I lifted my eyebrows.

'Right.' He laughed.

9:40 am

What just happened then, I asked myself? Did Mike Carmichael ask me out? Or was it a group kind of thing? Either way, I didn't care. He wasn't my type and I'd made a resolution never to be involved with anyone at work. It made life too complicated. Anyway, I hardly had time for relationships. I wanted Shelley's job by the time I was thirty. By then she'd have moved on. I knew the work it would take, and this promotion was the first step. No way was I going to let that jerk, Pete, take it from me. I turned back to my reading and note taking.

11:01am

Finished at last. I had a pretty good idea of the company policy now and where I wanted to take it. Shelley was right. It was out-dated and the onus was more on the employer to provide the opportunities rather than on the employee to seek them out. The two main components, as I saw them, were time and money. That had to shift from the employer to the employee. Anyone who wanted to keep their job or get ahead would have to show their commitment not only to the company but also to themselves. It would be easy to wrap it up in company-speak to show that it was a good thing — a necessary thing, a way-of-the-future thing. Even if you disagreed — which, face it, most people would because who wants to spend their own time and money attending boring courses — it would be hard to do so without looking like a slacker or a loser.

I stretched. Yeah, a bit of creative writing, that's what it needed and I was just the gal for that. I turned to the computer and stretched my fingers.

11:50am

I pressed print and looked around. Pete had left a few minutes ago and said he'd meet me there. Good. I didn't particularly want to walk with him. I wondered what he'd been up to during the morning. Of course we had our regular work to do too. Shelley had made that clear. I'd have to finish that file I started this morning before I went home tonight. Maybe I'd take it home with me.

12:04pm

Shannon's on Queen was half full with the early lunch crowd, but there were booths and that would give us a bit of privacy to talk – and fight if needs be. I found him in the corner booth, a Corona and a pile of papers in front of him. I got a diet Coke and joined him.

'Hey,' he said, looking up.

'Hey,' I answered and swung my briefcase on the table. For once I had no smart comeback. This felt so weird, being in a semi-social situation with Pete. It seemed he felt it too, so our awkwardness permeated the air. Jeez, I hated Shelley.

'Do you want to order anything to eat?' he asked.

'I'm not that hungry at the moment. You?'

'I'm good. Let's get started. Have a look at this.' He slid a sheet in my direction. 'The way I think we should go is the reflection angle. Look at your strengths, weaknesses and identify what you need to do to get better at your job. I've outlined a few ideas for the format of the pro forma.'

I quickly read over what he had written. 'This sounds more like a confession. Who the hell wants to tell their boss what their weaknesses are?'

'It's not about that. It's more like constructive self-analysis. If you do it correctly, it should be helpful.'

'Sounds too Dr Phil for me. I looked more at the time and money angle.' I outlined a few of my ideas.'

'That could work too. We've come at it from different directions, but combine the two and I'd say we had the perfect package.'

This sounded too easy and he was being way too nice. There must be a catch somewhere.

'Well, we have to look at the union angle too, you know. Make sure we don't infringe on anyone's rights, privacy etc.'

'Yeah, we should be okay on that. I've already run it by Shelley.'

'When?' My suspicions soared.

'This morning. I looked for you, but you weren't at your desk.'

'What did you do? Wait for me to go to the Ladies so you could rush in and tell Shelley all your great ideas?'

'My, what a nasty, suspicious mind you have. All I did was share a few ideas, check out the union angle and that. It's no big deal. As it happens she was more than receptive to my train of thought. Go talk to her this afternoon if you're that worried. You've got some good ideas.'

'Fuck off.'

'You really do have an anger management problem there, Kate,' he said and one corner of his mouth went up with the trace of a smile. Smug bastard.

'You really are a piece of work, you know that? You come across like Mr Congeniality, yet underneath it all you're as cunning as…as…' I was so angry I couldn't think, so I borrowed one of my dad's expressions, 'a shithouse rat.'

He laughed. 'Interesting turn of phrase there, kiddo. I've really learnt a lot about Australian lingo since I met you.'

I couldn't speak for a few minutes. This wasn't getting me anywhere. He was right about one thing. He did make me angry. I'd just have to learn to hide it more.

'Perhaps we should eat. We'll have to get back to the office soon.' he said.

Food was the last thing I felt like, but it would give me something to do while I thought about things. 'Okay, let's eat. You have to order at the counter.'

He got up, 'You stay here, save the booth – it's getting crowded now. What do you want?'

'Chef's salad,' I slid a twenty towards him, ' and another Coke.'

He shook his head, 'Don't worry. Hey, don't look daggers at me. I'm all for equality but for once, can't you let it go. You can pay next time, okay?'

'Fine, thanks.' Not that there would be a next time.

1:20pm

There were a few looks in our direction when we went back. I sure hoped Mike had let everyone know that Pete and I were working on a project together. Wouldn't want anyone to get the wrong impression.

We decided to both work on our own angles and bring it all together later on. It meant a late night, but I'd known that from the start. It also might mean working tomorrow. Shelley knew and expected that. How else would we get this finished by Monday?

4:00pm

My phone rang. It was Mum.

'Hi love. What time will you be coming tonight?'

Tonight? What was she talking about? 'I won't be coming over tonight, Mum. I have to work late. Why? Were you expecting me?'

'Expecting you! Of course, we're expecting you. Have you forgotten it's your brother's birthday tonight? Family barbecue, remember?'

Oh no. Craig was turning twelve and the whole family was coming. My sister, Laura, would be there along with her dropkick boyfriend, Troy. Gran and Granddad were driving down from the coast. How did I let it slip my mind?

'Sorry, Mum. Shelley gave me a project that has to be finished by Monday. There's no way I can come tonight. Tell Craig I'll get him an extra nice birthday present to make up for it.'

'Kate Elaine Higgins you are not missing your brother's birthday celebration! I don't care what you have to do, you can put it aside for one night.'

'But Mum, I really have to work.'

'Then do it tomorrow. You've worked on Saturday before, though why you can't work in a regular job with regular hours I don't know. Seems to me they take advantage of you at that company.'

I felt the frustration rising in me. Mum just didn't understand what businesses were like these days and that the only way to get to the top was to work harder, longer and smarter than everyone else. 'I'm working with another person, Mum. I can't just do my own thing here.'

'Fine, the more the merrier. Bring her along too. It'll do you both good to have a break. Then you'll be all the fresher for tomorrow.'

I screamed silently. My mother was the most stubborn, bossy woman I knew. 'It's a he, not a her, and there's no way Pete would want to go to a family party tonight.'

Pete just happened to stroll over at that moment. Talk about timing. He raised his eyebrows, and then said loudly. 'Pete would love to go to a family party with Kate tonight.'

Mum's voice practically sang. 'I heard that, Kate. See I was right. Pete sounds very nice. Tell him we're looking forward to meeting him. See you at seven, no later.' She hung up before I had a chance to answer. I slammed the phone on my desk.

'What did you do that for?'

Pete gave a choir-boy smile. 'Shelley wanted us to get to know each other. I can't think of a better way than meeting your family. Besides, we've got all weekend to work on this project.'

'Oh yeah, when am I going to meet your family, then?'

'London's a bit far for a weekend visit, but I'm sure they'd make you feel welcome.'

'How convenient for you. But you don't have to come to this thing, you know. In fact I'd rather you didn't.'

'Why ever not?'

'God, let me count the ways. We don't get along to put it mildly. We are rivals, enemies even. Truthfully, I hate your guts, Pete. Can I put it any plainer than that?'

'Subtlety was never one of your strengths, Kate. I must remember to put that down on your PD form. We are filling each other's out, remember?'

'Yeah, and I'll remember to put arrogance, sneakiness and underhandedness on yours.'

'Actually the last two are the same thing. But, seriously Kate, you have to go and if I tag along we may get a chance to talk about the project tonight. Kill two birds with one stone, if you know what I mean.'

'Have you any idea what you're getting yourself in for? It's my brother's twelfth birthday party and my whole family will be there.'

'Sounds delightful.'

'You're sick, you know that?'

'What time should I pick you up?'

I had the horrible feeling that he was just as stubborn as my mother. I contemplated just telling him to get lost. But he did have to fill out my PD form and I wouldn't put it past him to tell Shelley how uncooperative I had been. I didn't know whom I hated most at the moment, Shelley or Pete.

I scribbled down my address and handed it to him. 'I'll be leaving at 6:30, with or without you.'

'No problem! One more thing — what should I get your brother as a present?'

I smiled sweetly. 'Your head.'

'So cute.'

5:35pm

Finished this file at last. Just have time to zip home, have a shower and get ready. Why did my brother have to be born in January? Pete left five minutes ago with a jaunty, 'See you soon.' What the hell is he up to? He even told Shelley he was going to my parents' place. She beamed. Why bloody try? He's already got it in the bag. I closed my laptop. Most people had left, presumably for the wine bar. Seemed a better option at the moment.

6:00pm

Home. My studio flat in Paddington seemed so inviting tonight. I looked at the plasma TV and soft leather couch. Then I thought of Craig. He wasn't bad, for a kid, even if he was twelve years younger than me. There was a part of me that didn't want to disappoint him, that was glad I was going. If only Pete wasn't coming as well. Then a horrible thought hit me. I'd forgotten to get Craig a present. I meant to, but things had been so busy at work lately. I'd have to get a card at the local 7/11 and slip some money inside. Kids liked money, didn't they? I'd make it a hundred, that'd impress him.

6:25pm

I pulled on a pair of skinny jeans and a sleeveless red top, and then I applied minimal makeup. I wasn't out to impress anybody. I'd give him five minutes, and if he hadn't arrived, I'd leave. I sat down to watch the clock, hoping.

6:28pm

The doorbell rang. Damn. I got up and went to the door. There he was, showered— in jeans and a white shirt. He looked different, almost human. I'd never seen him in anything but a suit.

'Hi, you look nice,' he said.

Maybe he felt he had to say that. I decided to set the record straight. 'You don't have to say stuff like that, you know. This isn't a date.'

He laughed, 'God, I hope not.'

I felt relieved, and sort of insulted at the same time. 'Thanks,' I said dryly.

'Don't get me wrong. Nothing wrong with you, quite the opposite,' he said, giving me a look which made me a tad uncomfortable. 'But if this was a date, and I was meeting your parents for the first time, I'd be packing it.'

'You don't need to explain. Anyways, I'm ready. Let's go.' I turned off the lights and closed the door behind me. 'Oh, by the way, I need to pick up a card at the local shop.'

'You haven't gotten one yet?' He sounded surprised.

'Meant to but time just slipped away.' I hated sounding defensive and feeling guilty.

'I managed to get a computer game. Hope he's into that sort of stuff.'

'You mean you actually got him a present?'

'Of course. It is his birthday, after all.'

Jeez, was there nothing this man wouldn't do to show me up? If anyone told me twelve hours ago I'd be bringing Pete to meet my family I would have said they were nuts.

7:10pm

'Darling, good to see you.' Mum gave me a hug. Then she stepped back and eyed Pete. 'I'm so glad you could come. Peter, isn't it?'

'The pleasure's mine. I can see where Kate gets her looks from.'

Seriously? Couldn't he come up with something more original? The oldest line in the book and Mum fell for it, hook, line and sinker. She linked her arm in his and led him into the lounge. 'Here's Kate's young man, everyone. Peter...'

'Forest. Pete Forest.'

'And he's not my young man, he's a colleague from work!' I interjected, loudly.

Dad came over, good old Dad in too short shorts, a tee shirt and flip flops. He had a stubby in one hand and the barbecue tongs in the other. Great. All he needed was a plastic apron with boobs on it to complete the picture. He put the beer down and held out his hand. 'Welcome Pete. I'm Shane, Kate's dad. What can I get you?'

Pete shook his hand. 'Glad to meet you, Shane. A beer would be great.'

'Come on outside,' Mum said, 'and meet the others.'

The barbecue sizzled and the coloured lights, still up from Christmas, lit up the deck. Craig, already looking bored — after all what twelve year-old wants a family barbecue for his birthday — lit up when he saw me. That gave me a major guilt trip. I really should have remembered to get him a present.

'Hi, Sis.' He gave me an awkward hug and I tousled his hair. He was almost as tall as I was.

'Happy birthday, kid.' I passed him the envelope.

He opened it, 'Cool, thanks Kate.'

He looked impressed. At least I think he did.

'I thought you could buy what you wanted rather than get you something you have to pretend to like.'

'It's great.'

Pete handed him his present. It was wrapped even. 'Hope you like this. But you don't have to pretend, if you don't.' He laughed.

'Gee, thanks. You didn't have to, you know.'

'It's okay. I'm trying to impress your sister.' Pete smiled.

Craig tore off the wrapping. 'Vipers Nest, Part II! Awesome! It's just come out. You play too?'

'Sometimes. I have a brother about your age.'

'You want to try it later?'

'Craig, we're not going to be here that long. We've got work tomorrow.'

Craig shrugged, 'No worries, sis. Just being polite to your date and all, you know.'

'He's not my…'

'Kate, are you going to introduce us to your young man?' Grandma asked.

I gave up. I made the introductions to Grandma and Gramps. Then Laura, looking cool and sexy in a tight white dress, and Troy, looking like the jock he was, in a tighter white tee shirt, arrived. I made the introductions again.

Laura was in true flirt mode. 'I just love an English accent,' she said. 'What part of England are you from?'

'London, actually.'

I rolled my eyes and left them to it. I figured Pete was big enough to look after himself, even with someone like my sister.

I went in the kitchen to help Mum with the salad. 'He seems really lovely, darling,' she whispered. 'I'm so glad you brought him.'

'Mum, how many times do I have to say it? He's not my boyfriend! I hardly even know him. We are working on a project together. End of story.'

'Then why did he come tonight, if he's not interested in you?'

I said nothing but thought, yes, why did he come tonight? That's what worried me. We were rivals and nothing else. What was he up to? I'd been here fifteen minutes and already the night seemed too long.

8:15pm

Dinner. I decided, even though I loved my family (although the jury was out on Laura), they were a major embarrassment. They kept plying Pete with questions, which, I have to admit, he answered with a breezy politeness. I said as little as possible, stuck to Coke and kept glancing at my watch, wondering when we could go. We ate the steak, cut the cake and sang happy birthday to Craig. My mother insisted on these occasions and birthdays. Christmas, Australia Day and Easter were of course all celebrated and we were all expected to show up for duty. Usually, I accepted it with good grace, but tonight I wished I were elsewhere.

9:45pm

I was stacking the dishwasher and tidying up. Laura, slack ass, was supposed to be helping me but she was pretending to talk to Grandma. That girl would do anything to get out of work. Pete came in carrying glasses. 'You don't have to do that. You're a guest.'

'I don't mind.'

'Hey, I know your ulterior motive. You're just escaping the third degree from Mum and Grandma.'

He laughed, but didn't deny it.

'I warned you. The Higgins family is anything but subtle.'

'A bit like their daughter.'

'This is true. You know where you stand with me.'

'No doubt about that,' he said. I didn't like the serious look he gave me.

'Well, we ought to go soon. Early start in the morning, you know.'

'I'm ready when you are.'

I didn't like the way he said that either.

10:33pm

Home at last.

'You don't have to walk me to the door you know.' I said, as Pete started to get out of the car. 'This isn't a…'

'I know, Kate. This isn't a date. God, could you say it any more?' He sounded a bit weary.

I knew I should cut him some slack. He had behaved well all night. I asked myself again, why had he come at all? We hadn't talked business or anything. I was too tired to work it out.

I got out of the car and let him follow me to the door of my flat, without further argument. If he wanted to play the damn English gent, I'd let him. He leaned against the building as I opened the door. He looked as tired as I felt.

'Well, thanks for coming and for giving Craig a present and all,' I said.

'I enjoyed it.'

'Liar.' I said.

'Yeah, but the trouble is, you always catch me out.'

'Then how about trying the truth for a change?'

'The truth? You wouldn't believe it if I did.' He bounced his fist lightly against my chin. 'See you tomorrow, Kate.'

'What time?'

'Let's make it nine. After all it is the weekend.' He gave a wave and headed off towards his car.

I went inside and closed the door. Trying to undermine me with your charm, smartass? Don't bother.

10:55pm

He's up to something, I know it. I punched the pillow and closed my eyes.

II

Saturday

8:35am

Damn. I was meeting Pete at the office at 9:00 and I had slept in. So it looked like a takeaway coffee for breakfast as usual.

9:10am

The building felt strange on the weekend, empty, creepy. Security was there, of course. People sometimes went in on the weekend to catch up, Shelley especially, and they were used to us checking in on the odd Saturday.

9:16am

Pete was there already, of course. And surprisingly, so was Mike Carmichael.

'What are you doing here, Carmichael?'

His red head bobbed over the top of his laptop. 'Working, like you. Got a few things to catch up on. But I won't be here long. I won't spoil your date with Pete.'

'Shut up before I tip this coffee on you.'

'I wouldn't waste a perfectly good coffee on him,' Pete strolled over towards us. 'Not when I've got a couple of Danishes to go with it.' He dangled a paper bag from a local bakery in front of me.

I took a deep breath and suddenly felt hungry.

'Don't suppose you would have a third one there?' Mike asked hopefully.

'Love your optimism, Carmichael.' Pete laughed. 'Come on Kate, we may as well use the conference room where we can spread out stuff.'

'You better actually do some work in there. I'll be checking up on you two.' He called as we walked away.

'Get a life, Carmichael,' Pete said as he opened the door to the conference room. He'd already set up with his laptop and the paperwork he'd accumulated. I slung my laptop case across from him and set down my coffee.

He passed me a Danish and sat down, spreading his long, jean-clad legs out in front of him. He looked at me. 'You know, I had a good time last night. Your family is nice, welcoming.'

I sat down and took a bite of pastry. 'That's because they don't know you.'

'Yet.'

I raised my eyebrows. 'This project is only going to take the weekend. After that one of us is going to be the other one's boss. Have you forgotten that?'

'I'll be a very nice boss.'

I threw the empty bag at him, 'Dream on. And one thing more'

'What?'

'Have you forgotten that I don't like you?'

'Well, I've made progress. Yesterday you hated my guts.'

'Whatever, Forest. Let's just get on with it.'

12:03pm

We finally had a workable document and now it only needed fine-tuning. Pete had been less difficult to work with than I thought, and because we were covering different aspects of the policy, we only had one or two arguments.

'A couple of hours and it should be done,' I said, stretching.

'Lunch?'

'Or we could just push on and finish it.'

'You haven't forgotten we'll still have one more thing to do.'

'What?'

'We have to fill out each other's form. I have a feeling that's what Shelley will take the most notice of. What are we actually going to say about each other?'

'I forgot about that.' I had too. For a short while it had almost slipped my mind that Pete was the enemy, the stumbling block to me furthering my career.

'I have a suggestion. Why don't we just do our own forms? How the hell will Shelley know? Then we'll just read each other's so we know what's in it.'

I looked at him calculatingly. If he was on the level about this, it could be a good idea. We could be honest about ourselves, but not too honest and because we'd be reading each other's form, the temptation to jazz up our good points would be levelled out.

'Okay, fine with me. Naturally we won't tell Shelley.'

'What she doesn't know won't hurt her. This was a bitch of a thing for her to do anyway.'

I looked at him in surprise, 'Wow, bad language and criticism of the boss. Never thought I'd hear that from you.'

'Live and learn,' he said and smiled. 'Why don't we grab a sandwich, finish this off and go home. We can work on our forms and email them to each other tomorrow.'

'You know what? I never thought I'd say this, but for once I absolutely agree with you.'

'Still dislike me?'

'You bet.'

'Just thought I'd check. The universe is stable. By the way, Carmichael just left. Said to say good-bye. I think he likes you.'

'Be still my beating heart.' I fluttered my eyelashes for effect.

'Yeah, right.' He smiled as if he were pleased about something.

3:17pm

Press print. Finished. Hallelujah. Two copies, two forms. One for me, one for him. 'God, my brain feels numb.'

'I never want to see the words Professional Development again after this weekend. But we did good.' Pete gathered his papers and closed his laptop.

'Yeah, not bad, Forest. Just those forms to do. Sure you don't want me to help you fill out the bit about your weaknesses? I've got a list.'

'Cheeky as always, Higgins. Much as I'll miss your repartee I think I can manage.'

'My whatee? Jeez, Pete, speak English.'

'I thought I was. I keep forgetting Australians have a different approach to the Queen's English.'

'You want to watch that head of yours when you go out the door. It might not fit. But thank you for that. I needed reminding about what I hated about you.'

'Well, it's been fun for me too. 'He glanced at his watch. 'I have to go, just got time to make my train. Later, Kate.' A wave of the hand and he was out the door.

I sat for a moment. It was over and it hadn't been quite as bad as I feared. The worst part would be when Shelley handed down her decision.

7:25pm

Soaking in my bath, free from guilt now my form was finished. I hated these introspective things. I was more of an action and results girl. Still, I had tried to be honest, especially knowing that Pete was reading it. I shimmied down in the bath letting the warm sudsy water cover me.

7:45pm

I put on an old tee shirt and a pair of pyjama bottoms and towelled my hair dry for a few minutes. It was still a bit damp and would start to curl when it dried, but I couldn't care less. That was one of the joys of a Saturday night home alone. I could be a slob. I piled a plate with cheese and crackers, poured a glass of wine and settled on the sofa. I should be feeling great, I thought. Why this sudden flat feeling? I had thought Pete would suggest a drink or something to celebrate finishing the project. There had been the odd moment or two when I hadn't completely disliked him and we had worked well together. Not that I wanted to spend more time with him. But it kind of bugged me that he obviously felt the same way. I nearly laughed out loud at myself. Reality check, your nickname for him is 'Smartass'.

8:09pm

The doorbell rang. Pete was standing there with a bottle of champagne in one hand and a pizza balanced on the other.

'I decided I needed help filling in my form after all.'

I cocked my head on one side, 'Ever hear of the telephone?'

'Yeah, but I also needed someone to help me eat this.' He nodded at the pizza. 'You going to invite me in or what?'

'Do I have a choice?'

'Did I mention this was reef and beef?'

I opened the door wider. 'You certainly know one of my weaknesses. Come in.'

8:21pm

It was weird seeing Pete in my one armchair drinking bubbly and eating pizza. Unlike me, he was dressed nicely in cream shorts and a black tee shirt. I had fleetingly debated changing, but I didn't want to give the impression that his unannounced arrival should jolt me out of slob-mode in my own home. I ignored the fluttery butterfly feeling inside me. I resolutely put it down to hunger and not the male (who I had to admit was not exactly ugly) sitting across from me.

But this wasn't a date, I reminded myself. He probs just wanted to talk about our stupid forms and all. Still…he could have been anywhere else this evening and yet, he was here.

I went to get glasses and plates and to tell myself sternly that I wasn't the least bit affected by him. Yes, he was being nice, but he probably had an ulterior motive. He always did. Good, I thought, that's it, concentrate on his faults, his many faults.

I sat down on the sofa and he opened the pizza box, and passed it to me.

'So, don't you have a girlfriend or something to help you eat this?' was the stupid question I asked before I could stop myself.

He shrugged and said, 'Who has the time? Besides, I've only been over here a year, and I actually haven't met that many people. What about you? What are you doing on your own on a Saturday night? Oh, of course, waiting for me to show up.' He grinned.

I tossed a pillow at him. 'Very funny, not. I should have thought the answer to that was obvious last night with the way Mum and Grandma pounced on you and gave you the third degree. No one for a while. I'm more of a career girl. The guy I — sort of — went out with a couple years ago didn't get that.'

'Sounds a bit of a Neanderthal, if you don't mind my saying.'

'Don't mind at all – it's more polite than what I called him.'

'I thought you reserved those sorts of names for me.'

'Nah, I'm very generous with my insults.' I looked at him. 'I can overdo it sometimes. This was nice of you.' I pointed at the pizza box.

'I have an ulterior motive.'

'I knew it.' I wasn't surprised but...I think my heart skipped a beat. Jeez, what was wrong with me tonight? I tried to assume my usual tone with him. 'What is it? Spill, Forest.'

He put his glass down and did that crooked thing with his mouth that passed for a smile. 'Well, you certainly gave me a list of my faults. But what about my good points? I could do with a bit of help there.'

'And you're asking me, your number one fan — not.'

'At least you'll be honest.'

'What if I can't think of any?'

'Try — you'd have to put something down if you were filling out the form for me.'

'Okay, let me concentrate. This will take some hard thinking.' I closed my eyes and furrowed my brow for effect. 'Right,' I opened my eyes and looked at him in his clean, pressed clothes. 'You're very neat.'

'That's it? Sounds almost a fault the way you say it.'

'Hmmm. You buy nice food.'

'A little better — you could have added generous and thoughtful.'

'Let's not get carried away here. I suppose I could say you are usually polite, except when you're insulting me.'

'I never have!'

'Yes, in a sneaky way you have, but that's on the other list. And you have a sort of nice smile.' Why had I said that? Even if it was true.

'Now we're getting somewhere. What else?'

'That'll do for now.' And then, without even trying I realised I could have added a few more things, way more personal; like how I suddenly noticed he was pretty well built and his after shave was subtle but spicy. But that was getting onto dangerous ground. And yet, I couldn't help wonder what Pete thought about me. There was something about the way his intense brown eyes looked in my direction that made me ask, 'What are my good points?'

'I need another drink to work that out.'

'Gee, thanks. It doesn't count if you're drunk.'

'I am not going to get drunk. I have to drive home.'

'Right, upward citizen and all that.' I filled his glass and topped mine up.

He took a sip and then said, 'You're funny. A bit crass sometimes, but funny. And, you tell it like it is with no filters.'

'I think of that as one of my better qualities, though I prefer the word frank…or perhaps outspoken.'

'You do have a way with words. Your part of the policy was well written.'

'Thank-you.'

'You're welcome. And you're smart.'

'Sure you don't mean a smartass?'

'I thought that name was reserved for me. You're not good with compliments, are you?'

I shrugged my shoulders, starting to feel increasingly uncomfortable, yet very aware of Pete's presence so close to me.

'Try this one then. You're really nice looking, in fact, I might even say beautiful.'

I looked down at my glass really hard. Okay, so I had a feeling where this was heading…but did I want it? The ground between us had shifted. But, what was happening now? I hated the way my palms were starting to sweat and the strange excitement that was building in the pit of my stomach. I didn't feel in control anymore and that scared me most of all.

'What?' he said and leant over to tweak one of the now curly strands of my hair. 'No smart come back? Don't tell me I've made you speechless?'

I looked up at him sideways, 'I think you're drunk, Forest.'

He laughed and slid over on the couch next to me. 'Yeah, a glass and a half of wine goes straight to my head. Don't take advantage of me now.' His arm dropped around my shoulder. Why didn't I move away? I must be in a state of shock, I decided.

'Pete, what's going on here?' My words were coming out all breathy.

'Well, I think I'm going to kiss you, if you don't mind.'

And that's when I should have made it clear right there and then that no way was I going to fraternise with the enemy. But the mind and the body aren't always in sync. This was one of those times. Before I could stop myself I said, 'What are you waiting for then?'

9:45pm

Sometimes, thinking can be highly overrated. I discovered that kissing could definitely be put on Pete's list of good points. As I snuggled into him, he put his chin on my head and played with my hair. Apparently he thought my tousled lion's mane attractive.

'I always thought your insults were a way of attracting my attention. It worked too.'

I looked up at him indignantly. 'Don't flatter yourself, Forest. I'm just using you now, you know, for your body.'

'Yeah. I'm just a chick-magnet. I knew you wouldn't be able to resist me.'

I dug him in the ribs with my elbow.

'Ow, that hurt. Play nice now.'

'Chick-magnet indeed. You know, I could have guys if I wanted them. I am not unattractive.'

'Seem to remember telling you that. And yes, Carmichael would come running if you crooked your finger at him. But the fact is I'm here with you right now. That's not so bad, is it?'

I allowed my finger to trace his jaw and run over his lips. He grabbed my hand and kissed it, then he moved to my neck, my chin and finally my lips. 'You'll do,' I whispered and returned his kiss.

12:03am

Pete left. Reluctantly (after all he was pretty hot and I was tempted) but firmly, I told him it was time to go. And like the gentleman I'd assumed he was pretending to be but actually was, he went. It was nice just making out. Pete didn't push it, and I was relieved. I couldn't go from hating a guy one day to sleeping with him the next. I made us tea and we talked, like real people for a change. I found out he missed home, his family, England. He had been transferred here from the head office in London. It was too good an opportunity to miss and so he had worked hard and tried to get ahead. How ironic that if he succeeded it would be at my expense. But I didn't hold it against him anymore. It was a level playing field now. Whoever won, won.

12:23am
Wish I could get to sleep. Wish I wasn't wishing that Pete was here now.

III

Sunday

9:01am

The insistent ringing of my phone woke me up. I picked it up from the bedside table.

'Hello?' I mumbled, half asleep.

'Miss me yet?'

Consciousness slowly returned. 'Pete?'

'None other! What are you doing?'

'Sleeping until just a minute ago.' I sat up in bed and looked at the bedside alarm clock. 'Jeez, I can't believe it's after nine. I must have slept like a log.'

'That's probably because you had such a wonderful, relaxing evening, followed by even more wonderful dreams. I hope I was in both.'

'Steady on. It's more likely because I had too much wine last night and not enough sleep last week.'

'Quite the romantic, aren't you? Anyway…on to more practical matters. Do you want to do something today?'

'Well I thought I might do some laundry, buy some groceries and call Mum.'

'I meant with me. You can do those other things any time, except for calling your mother. I'm sure you can fit that in around whatever we decide to do.'

'Sheesh, you're getting ahead of yourself, boy! I haven't said yes yet.'

'Should I call back when you've woken up more?'

'Might be an idea. I'm not good in the morning.'

'You make up for it at night.'

'Shut up.'

'Love it when you talk tough.'

9:45am

The phone rang. 'Hi again. Awake yet?'

I looked at the coffee cup in my hand. 'I'm still on my first coffee. You don't give a girl much time.'

'Well the day's slipping away. What would you like to do? Go to the beach?'

'Too hot, too crowded. It's school holidays.'

'Well, then a movie? It's air conditioned.'

'Nothing's out I want to see.'

'Suggestions?'

'Let's keep it simple. A picnic at the Botanic gardens in the city. There might be an open air concert or something. I'll get some stuff together. But seriously, I need to do a few things around here this morning. I'll meet you there around noon.'

'I'll pick you up.'

'No, parking's too hard to get. Take the train, it's easier.'

'Not trying to ditch me already are you?'

'Of course not. I'm just being practical. See you then.'

9:50am

I was. Trying to run away that is. This thing with Pete was moving too fast for my liking. I needed time to process things. Relationships complicated everything, especially when you worked with someone. And this particular relationship, if that's what it was, could prove to be very toxic. I couldn't forget we were in competition for the same job. There were bound to be feelings when one of us didn't get it. Best to cut it now before we got in too deep. I would text him at noon and let him know I couldn't make it. Yes, that would be better for all concerned. I felt relieved. After all there was no way I could have a relationship with Pete Forest. What was I thinking last night?

10:50am

I hung out my washing in the communal yard for our flats. Was I being unfair? Under different circumstances,

I could probably go out with him. But…two days ago I hated him. How could I do a 180 degree turn in such a short time? I was doing the right thing in stopping this before it got started.

11:59am

Was it too late to change my mind? Was I throwing away something that could be really good? Maybe I was too focussed on my career? Bite your tongue, girl. You've worked your arse off in that company and now you're acting like some love struck teenager with her first boyfriend.

12:03pm

I sent the text and now I felt like shit. But it was the best thing to do, for both of us.

12:20pm

No reply. What did I expect?

1:10pm

I'll watch that DVD. I didn't get a chance to last night. It'll take my mind off things.

3:30pm

Gawd, I hate Sundays. Perhaps I'll do my ironing for the week. Get ahead, be organised.

4:15pm

Geez, I haven't emailed my form to Pete yet. Should I bother? Has he sent his to me? I'll check. Nope. He must really be angry with me. Guess I'll just have to hope for the best with Shelley.

8:30pm

It's not too early to go to bed, surely? I do need a lot of sleep and I want to be fresh in the morning. I don't want to face Pete tomorrow. But we both have to be civil and give our report to Shelley. I can do that surely.

8:35pm

My phone rang. I nearly dropped it I was so quick to pick it up. 'Yes?'

'Kate, Pete here.'

'Oh Pete, I'm sorry. Please let me explain.'

'No, it's fine. I'm cool with it. I just rang to say I'm going to tell Shelley I no longer want the promotion. In fact I no longer want the job. I'm returning to England after I've worked out my notice.'

'What? You can't be serious.'

'Yes, actually, I am.'

'But why? Look if you're pissed off with me, I can understand that. But it shouldn't stop you from going for the job if you want it.'

'That's the point. I no longer want it. You did me a favour really. I didn't realise, until this weekend, how much I was giving to work and how little to myself. It's crazy you know, putting work before everything else. That's no way to live. And when I went to your parents' house on Friday night, it was so nice and normal, it made me realise how much I miss that. And the way I treated you and everybody else at work – I didn't like the person I had become. I don't want to be like Shelley in ten years time. I'd rather have a life.'

'Oh,' I didn't know what to say. Of all the things I thought he might say, this never entered my mind. 'But Pete, think about this. You might change your mind in the morning. I'm really sorry if I made you feel this way. I feel like a jerk.'

'Don't. You probably did the right thing for you. You don't want a relationship with anyone at the moment, and certainly not with me. I get that. Anyway, I think you'll make a fine boss.'

'Oh Pete, I didn't want it this way.'

'Be honest, kiddo, you wanted it any way you could get it. And I think that means you're the best person for the job. You win.'

Tears started to stream down my face. I didn't feel like a winner.

'Pete?'

'Yeah?'

'Do you hate me?'

'Of course not. Hey, are you crying?'

I took a breath. 'Me? Certainly not. I'm as tough as nails, Forest.'

'You are that. See you tomorrow, Kate.'

'Bye.' I put the phone down and burst into tears.

IV

Monday

7:00am

I lingered over my coffee. I'd had a long, bad night. Pete's words had swirled in my mind incessantly. I thought about everything he'd said, and somewhere in the middle of the night, after tossing and turning and tangling my sheet in a knot, I realised something huge. I realised I didn't want to be like Shelley either. I wasn't even sure I wanted the job anymore, let alone the promotion. For the past couple of years it was like I had been sucked into a vortex, where the only thing that mattered had been work. Hell, I'd even forgotten my twelve year-old brother's birthday. I was only twenty-four and yet for the last two years I'd hardly gone out and I hadn't had a holiday. No wonder I'd fallen into Pete's arms so easily. It had been a long while since anyone had held me, touched me, kissed me. And it had felt nice, felt right with Pete. My body had more sense than my brain. He was not the person I thought he was. I could really fill in that list now with all his good points. He was kind, thoughtful and even funny, in his British sort of way. In fact, I kind of liked him — a lot. But it was too late. Or was it?

8:10am

Nearly everyone was there when I walked in the office. Pete waved and smiled at me, ever polite, even now. I smiled back, but headed for my desk. I didn't want to talk to him. At least, not yet.

8:25am

Shelley burst through the doors making her usual dramatic entrance, and then disappeared into her office. The report was on her desk already. I'd put it there after I'd arrived this morning, along with the forms we'd filled in. I guessed at some point in the day she would call us in.

9:00am

I saw Pete go into her office. Probably he wanted to tell her his decision and hand in his notice. I wondered briefly if he had changed his mind. But I quickly dispelled that. No, not after what he said last night.

11:05am

After that first early wave and smile, neither Pete nor I had said anything to each other. It was funny, but I missed him. Even the insults we traded were better than this.

Noon

I wish she would get it over and done with. Carmichael had been chirping around the office like a bird all morning. He must have had a good weekend.

12:15pm

Shelley came to her office door and called out, 'Pete, Kate, could you come into my office for a minute.'

We walked in and sat in the two chairs she indicated. Our Professional Development document was sitting on her desk. She tapped it, 'You've both done an excellent job on this. It's very thorough and addresses the very things I outlined to you on Friday. Well done.'

'Thanks,' I said. Pete was silent.

'I've also looked at the forms you filled out for each other. Pretty honest stuff. I'd say you both got a chance to know each other better this weekend.'

This time it was me who said nothing.

'It was a valuable experience,' Pete said.

'So it would seem,' Shelley said. 'You may or may not know, Kate, that Pete has withdrawn his application for the promotion, for personal reasons. He wants to go back to England. So the job is yours. Congratulations. I'll make the recommendation at our next board meeting.'

Pete turned to me and held out his hand, 'Yes, congratulations Kate.'

I took his hand and squeezed it. I remembered the first time I had shaken hands with him on Friday. Today his hand was still warm and firm and the smile was genuine. But now, it felt so different. I wanted more.

Shelley held out her hand too, but I ignored it. 'Thank you Shelley, but your congratulations are a little premature. You see I've also had time to think this weekend and I've decided I don't want the job either.'

Pete sat up in his chair.

'Really?' She looked at me in surprise. 'After all this work, I'd be interested in knowing the reason why.'

'I guess that's the problem. I've been working too hard. I nearly missed my brother's birthday party because of this and I really don't want that to happen again. And another thing, I'd like to take a little time off, which wouldn't be fair if I were to take on a new job.'

'Time off?' Shelley frowned.

'Yes, I haven't had a holiday in two years so I have quite a bit of leave accumulated.'

'Oh, I see. So you're putting your career ambitions on hold for a while?' Her tone was quite sharp.

'You could say the ambitions are turning in a different direction.'

Shelley stood up, 'Well, I hope you know what you're doing, both of you. Opportunities like this don't come along very often you know.'

I looked at Pete and smiled. 'Yes, I know.'

12:30pm

I was sitting in Shannon's with Pete having lunch.

'Well, it looks like we'll both have some time on our hands soon,' I said.

'You're just taking some leave, aren't you? You're not quitting or anything.' He tilted his head on one side and gave me one of those looks that I couldn't read.

'I don't know. I guess I'll have to think about that.' I gave him a half smile.

'Where are you going for a holiday?'

'That depends.'

'On what?'

'What's the weather like in England in February?'

He made his crooked little smile. 'Lousy, but of course the continent is much better.'

'Trouble is I might need a tour guide. Someone who knows their way around.'

'I think I might know just the guy.'

'Will he be free do you think?'

'I guarantee it.' He leaned across the table and kissed me.

1:30pm

We walked back to the office feeling elated. We still had a month left here and already we had planned a few of our weekends. Mum, I warned him, would insist on at least one more family meal. 'She's very bossy, you know.'

'Not unlike someone else.'

'I'm not bossy, I'm …'

'Delightful,' he kissed the top of my head before we turned towards our building.

'Yeah, right,' I replied, lamely. It seemed being happy had a detrimental effect on my sarcasm.

1:35pm

We went through the swing doors to the office. Mike Carmichael walked towards us with a huge grin on his fact.

'Hey, guess what?'

'What's up Carmichael?' Pete asked.

'Shelley called me into her office. I just got a promotion. I'm going to be your new boss.'

Pete and I looked at each other and burst into laughter.

'Good luck, Mike. You just might need it,' Pete said, as he put his arm around me.

Acknowledgements

Kudos and gratitude to all those who helped make this little book happen. Special thanks to my family; to Rob, who supports me in everything I do; to Ruth, who reads, edits and helps in more ways than I can mention; and to Richard, who encourages and cheers me on. Also thanks to my many writer friends, who have inspired, helped and taught me so much, particularly those at WriteLinks and the Rainforest Writers' Retreat members. A final tip of the hat to Anthony and the team at the Self Publishing Lab, who always make my books look fantastic.

I hope you enjoyed *High Stakes*, the first novella in Short Sweetz, a series of stand alones, full of heart and humour. Perfect if you want something to read in a session, either on the train, having a coffee, or whenever you can grab an hour or two away to escape.

If you have the time, I would love it if you could leave a review of the book either on Amazon or Good Reads.

Coming soon!

Bonjour Cherie
#2 in Short Sweetz

It's Paris or bust in this comedy of errors about seeing beneath the surface. Beth Jenkins is into all things French, especially her French teacher, Andre LeBlanc. She's on the fast track to Paris, and nothing will stop her, not even the very Australian, Zac Mills, who always seems to turn up when she's in the most trouble. As she endeavours to catch Andre's interest, she also ignores the growing chemistry with Zach. But, as mishap after mishap delays her dreams, Beth begins to learn that neither Andre nor Zac are quite what she thinks. Will it be too late to win the one man who shows her that Paris is not the only destination worth planning for?

About the author

Robin Martin has been a writer and a teacher for many years. Originally from Canada, she has lived and worked in several countries, but now lives just outside Brisbane, Australia. Writing has always been her passion, and in recent years she has written several novels for young adults and adults, including *The Alien Chronicles*, and *The Short Sweetz* series.

When she is not plotting stories, she loves reading everything from cereal boxes to long novels she can get lost in. She finds her inspiration in long walks along the beautiful Queensland coast, listening to an eclectic music collection that ranges from The Rolling Stones to Mozart, and good coffee, without which she wouldn't be able to function.

Visit Robin at *www.robinmartinthomas.com* to find out about her other works and to sign up for her newsletter to receive free stories and the latest updates on her next books. You can also check out her author Facebook page at https://www.facebook.com/robinmartinthomas or follow her on Instagram @georgi_two_martini

www.ingramcontent.com/pod-product-compliance
Lightning Source LLC
Chambersburg PA
CBHW032011120726
47902CB00014B/2082